BALCONIES

Barry Upton

Two novellas which bring murder and mystery to popular holiday islands.

Balconies first appeared as two separate novellas, the first published in 2015, the second in 2017. They are brought together here in this new and revised edition.

BALCONIES

Malta

How would you spend your last day on a beautiful Mediterranean island?   Plotting murders perhaps?

A thriller in six acts.

A beautiful woman plots the murder of her husband and then sets plans in motion to destroy all the evidence.

BALCONIES

ONE

THE WOMAN, VALLETTA

The Woman looks again in the mirror, at her lips, perfectly drawn, perfectly red, which she purses slightly and approves. It is early for her, but she always looks good. The clock behind her shows the time in reverse. She turns away from the ornate frame and notes the money, stacked high on the table; used notes, set out into five piles. There is enough in each of them to leave the island and start again in Sicily. To leave the old life behind. Slowly she gathers each pile and puts them on top of each other. Now there is just one pile. And more to come. She smiles.

BALCONIES

The woman returns to her computer and starts to type. She looks again at the message, sends it, closes the lid, and awaits the first telephone call.

Outside, beyond the balcony, the sun is already hot and the air humid. The day will get hotter.

BALCONIES

TWO

THE SHOOTER, ST PAUL'S BAY

When the letter arrived, leaning up against the door of his second-floor apartment, into which he'd just moved, it brought with it a sense of excitement. On closer inspection, while the address was undoubtedly his, the addressee was definitely not him. The name on the envelope was *Antony Sammett*. He must have been a former tenant. How disappointed Paul felt, as though he'd found a penny and lost a pound, or perhaps that should have been a cent and a euro. He was getting used to the new currency.

BALCONIES

Malta was his new home, at least for the foreseeable future. He hoped that this time he would be able to settle somewhere, after living the nomadic life for so long. He blamed nobody but himself for that. His decisions had made him a wanderer. The weather was glorious and the view from his balcony spectacular. Ok, so the money was different, but at least they drove on the left and - mostly - spoke English; a home from home, without the incessant summer rain he'd willingly left behind in Warrington. The bright blue sky burst into view through the balcony windows as he opened the apartment door that led onto the balcony. He slid both French doors open, closed the front door behind him and stood, as he'd done so often in the past seventy-two hours, basking in the warmth, enjoying the peaceful sight of the multi-coloured luzzu fishing boats bobbing on the gentle Mediterranean. Even from here he could see the eyes, painted on to either side of the prow, inviting him to sea. It was a great view, but the apartment was a temporary stop. Once he had the money he'd been promised, he would find somewhere more luxurious, perhaps in one of the busier, trendier places. This apartment had been given to him on his arrival. Rent paid for four weeks.

He turned back into the apartment, through the door, leaving it open behind him. Soon it would be too warm, but for now he could enjoy the view. He threw the letter onto the table, collected up the detritus from an earlier breakfast, and went to

BALCONIES

the kitchen. He dumped the crockery and cutlery into the sink, moved across to the fridge and poured himself another iced tea. He had taken to iced tea. "The Englishman abroad makes few compromises", he said aloud. Iced tea was close enough for him.

The letter sat there, unopened, tempting him, but for now there were other things to do. He plugged in his computer, waited for it to start up, impatient for the desktop-laden icons to appear, one by one, like drops of rain in a summer shower. Then the familiar ping. The email had arrived. He read it through, then again, just in case there was something not clear about the instructions. He made a mental note of time and place, and then discarded it into the bin. He thought again about how odd this new-speak of ours was. Bins for discarded emails. Where do they go, when they are emptied, he wondered - these messages of hope, of announcement, of downright dull? To a recycling plant somewhere? Who would re-use them? What would they become? He closed the lid.

When he looked up, it was still there, the unopened letter, taunting him. He picked it up and looked again at the name: *Antony Sammett,* turned it over in his hand, felt the weight and length of it. He knew he really shouldn't open it. He should pass it on to the landlord - landlady? He'd only spoken once to her; he didn't even know where she lived. He slid his finger behind the sealed flap. The letter was clearly addressed to someone else, and it was clearly, too, a business letter of some

BALCONIES

sort. Inside there was a simple business card, but blank. No heading. No name. No address. No numbers. Just on one side, in pencil, was sketched a picture of a lion's head, and beneath it three letters, in capitals: **J A C**.

Jac... Perhaps it was a name. Or just a cryptic message to Antony Sammett, which only he and the sender would understand. It would never make any sense to him, the unintended reader. And, he wondered, what about the lion's head? Storylines flitted through his head to make some sense of the cryptic message:

Jac was short for Jacqueline. Jackie Lyon, the girl with whom Antony had shared the flat before an argument had driven her out, in a temper, fed up with his lascivious leers and groping hands...

JAC was an acronym: Jerome and Company, specialist wine merchants to the Doges of Venice, who waited for Antony Sammett, their customer, to collect his order...

No. It would never make any sense to him! It was never intended for his eyes. He put the card back into the envelope, with a sigh. It would be nice if he got a letter. But who would send him one? No-one at home knew where he was. It was safer that way. And, more than anything, he wanted to feel safe. He put the card back into the envelope, felt it settle back into its preformed place, folded the flap down and left it there.

1015 - Bugibba Square: easy enough to remember. He went into the bedroom, opened the bottom drawer, took out his

BALCONIES

small brown leather bag, and checked the notes again. The amount was exactly what he'd been told to bring. There would be no negotiations, the caller had said, with her familiar voice: Mediterranean, slightly hoarse and deep. Once again he conjured up the image he had in his head of her: red lipstick on pouting mouth, long hair swept back, dyed the ubiquitous deep auburn that Maltese women shared. Would *she* be there? He doubted it. No, there would be someone else to do the pick-up, a go-between.

He had first heard her voice six months before he arrived in Malta. The job she was offering had been outlined to him. It seemed bold and dangerous but he had already determined to leave England and this was his way to pay off all his debts and start a new life somewhere hot and exotic. Or so Malta seemed to him. Waving guns around in front of shopkeepers had lost its allure. It was only a matter of time before he was caught. When he had arrived at the airport there had been a driver waiting for him, a brief sound of Eastern European, waving a makeshift card with his name printed bold and large. He had been taken to St. Paul's Bay and given the keys. The driver outmanoeuvred other mad drivers, one hand on the wheel, the other gesturing wildly. There had been a mobile phone on the seat next to him. It rang and the chauffeur's eyes had directed him to answer it. Her voice. Her welcome. Her instructions.

BALCONIES

The job itself had gone well enough. CCTV was disabled. The man was alone in the hotel room - The Excelsior, he recalled, a posh place - just as she'd said he would be. The balcony door had been open - he remembered that, too - and noises from the street drifted into the room. As he pulled out the gun, already prepared, with silencer to muffle the deadly report, the man had fallen to his knees, had begged him, offering him all the money in his suitcase. Paul had raised the gun, held it to the kneeling man's temple and fired it. The pop was drowned out by the sounds of shouting from the noisy pool terrace below. He had watched the man fall onto his side, his knees still folded. He grabbed the suitcase, pushed the gun in amongst the bundles of euros, zipped up the bag and slowly, casually sauntered out of the hotel. Piece of piss!

He returned to the balcony, watching the queue of tourists forming along the harbour wall, waiting to climb onto one of the boats that would take them round the bay to Comino. The sun made the water sparkle, and he breathed it all in. He looked at his watch. Just twenty minutes to go. Then all of this would be over and he would be free to find a place of his own. And rich enough to pay for it. A boat's klaxon sounded. It was time to go. He left the front door ajar as he'd been told. "The money will be there when you return. In a pile. On the table." He grabbed the package from the bottom of

BALCONIES

the wardrobe where it had lain all this time, the money taken from the hotel.

"Packet for a packet," a man said. This was Paul's cue. It was the Eastern European accent again. Probably one of the Bulgars or Russians who filled up the hotels and apartments, or waited on tables and shook cocktails.
"Packet for a packet, my friend," Paul responded, as he'd been instructed. And the man patted Paul on the shoulder for all the world to see, like old friends meeting for a pint and a soccer match. He held tightly onto his small shapeless bundle and Paul fished his own from the brown bag, handing it to him. The man held it in his hand, weighing it...
"It's all there."
The man passed Paul his package. It was heavy in his hand. He put it into the bag.
"We trust you. She trusts you. Otherwise I would not be here." And then he wasn't. The gun was Paul's and the money was gone.

BALCONIES

THREE

THE CHAUFFEUR, IL-MDINA

It was hot. It was always hot.
Antony Sammett stood staring out of the balcony window. From here, above the streets, he watched as the tourists flocked in and around the old city streets. Mdina was hot. The flat was hot, Antony was hot. Even this early in the morning he could feel the beads of sweat on his forehead, on his hands, on his back. From his viewpoint he saw their heads, crisscrossing the street below as they touched the golden walls and admired the wide range of handles and knockers that adorned the brightly coloured doors lining the street. Mdina

BALCONIES

was busy but it was safer here. And Antony needed to feel safe.

He had dressed early, ready (for what exactly?) for over an hour. The email had arrived, just as she had said it would. Short and to the point. Unlike the last one she had sent, where she had clearly been mad at him for changing her plans. He hated it at St. Paul's Bay, with the hot sun shining onto the open balcony, and the smell of cats everywhere. It was impossible to be anonymous there. A friend - from school some fifteen years ago - had left his flat here in *The Silent City*, so he'd vacated the apartment opposite Bugibba Harbour: bright, noisy, exposed, and taken this one: dark, quiet, hidden from view. So she'd been mad.

"I've already sent you instructions to the apartment in Bugibba... I shall send them again to you there. From now on, stick to the plans, Mr Sammett, if you please."

He could tell he'd pissed her off. She hung up, left him clutching at the cell phone which had been left for him there. She left no time to reply, to explain. The bitch. Still, he'd done what he wanted and now he was feeling a little easier here in this borrowed flat in a tourist hot-spot in anonymity.

More heads passed below him, occasionally looking up to admire an ornate street lamp or an elaborately carved balcony. Then on their way they went, to pick through the glass trinkets in the shops, or to dine on cakes at The Cafe Fontanella, built into the city walls looking out across the Dome of Mosta and

BALCONIES

beyond to the sea glinting blue beyond. Let them go and have their fun, these transients, making their pilgrimage to the sights of the island. He would wait here until the last possible moment. Out of the heat.

J A C and the lion's head, all printed in blue. It would mean nothing to anyone else, but to him the message was clear enough. The car, a blue Peugeot, with the registration letters JAC would be waiting in the car park outside the city walls, keys left in the same place. His mind travelled back to the last time she'd sent a message. A different code, a different car, but the same meaning. The destination and the job details had been attached to the steering wheel. All that was required of him that time was to deliver the bag on the back seat to the Excelsior Hotel in Floriana, leave the keys in the car and take the bus back to Bugibba. He'd not set foot inside the hotel. He'd only seen it from the ferry boat that took him from Sliema to Valletta. He'd been tempted to touch the bag, feeling for its contents. As soon as his fingers felt the cold shape of it, he withdrew them again. The package was none of his business. What would be expected of him this time, this last time? She'd promised him: this was the last time she would use him. Then he would get the money; she had promised. Then Antony Sammett could do what he liked. Perhaps he'd be able to buy a place in one of the shady streets of Valletta. He looked again at his watch. The sweat on his back made him feel uncomfortable. The shirt stuck to him and for the

BALCONIES

umpteenth time that morning, he tugged it clear of his sticky back.

What had been in that bag? He'd not looked at it. He'd been told in a way that made it very clear, the phone bristling with menace from an Eastern European voice, that he was not to open it. She would never have known. Or perhaps she would. Had she had him watched. The voice suggested a man who would bring violent retribution. She would have no hesitation in using his brutality . Antony Sammett was sure of that. But he wished he'd had enough courage. But courage was not in his DNA. He felt the sweat on his back again at the thought of it. So, he had done as he'd been told. Drive and leave. Exactly that. This job would be the same he supposed. Drive and leave, then a bus back. Just a few hours later the money would arrive.

But what if it didn't? What if she had been stringing him along all this time, the bitch, with her silky voice and her menacing Russian heavy. If that was the case, he had his insurance policy. Antony Sammett would know what to do, who to talk to, if she betrayed him. He needed that money. She'd promised him a better life, and he was determined to have it. He'd buy a car of his own, that was the first thing he'd do. A swanky car to go with a swanky apartment. No more driving other people around.

BALCONIES

It was nine-thirty. Somewhere outside in the city, deep chimes rang the half-hour, and he took a last long look out of the balcony window. Even at this time the streets were full. The horses, drawing their carriages, with their clip-clopping hooves, the sounds echoing from the walls. He slipped on a clean white shirt, the chauffeur's uniform, throwing his discarded one into the corner with the rest. He stood facing the mirror, and looked into the eyes of the man who faced him. He saw the beard, prematurely greying, and tried a smile. It was not a success. Soon there'd be plenty to smile about.

He pulled the door behind him, took the stairs slowly, one step at a time - he was a cautious man - and emerged into the shadows of the city. The yellow walls were cool, and silent, sucking in the heat and noise, throwing out nothing. He made his way to the Greek Gate, passing very few tourists in these quieter streets, crossed the bridge and glanced down into the green-lawned moat. The smell of the horses made the air thick and unpleasant and flies buzzed about his head. He crossed the road, picking his way through the parked buses disgorging their passengers into the gardens. A brief glance round the car park and he found the car - a blue Peugeot, JAC 906. He knelt to re-knot his lace, felt the top of the tyre - off-side rear as usual - and with the keys he opened the door and slid into the front seat. He looked around him, trying to appear nonchalant, normal, despite the sticky nervousness. Was she here, watching him? Had she delivered the car

BALCONIES

herself? Of course she hadn't. Another would have done it. A go-between. The Russian perhaps with his menacing voice and heavy fists? How many of them were there? All doing as she asked. It didn't matter. None of it mattered. Soon it would be all over and then Antony Sammett would be rich. Very rich.

The yellow post-it was stuck onto the steering wheel, as before. He smiled in recognition of the destination and turned the key. He drove away from the city and downhill to join the Mosta traffic as he headed towards Valletta. He felt the slipping, sliding motion of the car as the tyres lost their grip in the heavy shower of rain that fell onto the hot tarmac. His foot moved across to cover the brake pedal.

BALCONIES

FOUR

THE ENGINEER, BIRGU

Adrian jingled the coins in his pocket. Bastards! Filthy rich arrogant bastards. All of them. Well let them all wait; he'd show them. Let them wait until he had his money. Then they'd see.
Every day he watched them, with their blue-and-white striped shirts and their faux admirals' caps; he watched them from the balcony he shared with his neighbours. His tiny room overlooked the sea wall at Kalkara, but he would have to give it up soon. The developers had moved in, and the whole block would be demolished. Not before time, in truth, to make way for the new elegant apartments. The designs were posted on

BALCONIES

billboards outside the front door that served the eight rooms over three storeys that he and seven others shared, reminding them that better days were ahead but *they* would not be part of them. Well, we'd see. He'd have the money soon, and he *would* be able to afford one of their poxy flats, if he wanted!

His wallet was empty now, but all that would be put right soon. Very soon. She had promised. He'd long since stopped using a wallet as he had nothing but a few coins to put in it. Meals came from the generosity of his neighbours. It was not a wallet he felt, alongside the coins, it was the screwdriver, his forefinger caressing the point while his fist wrapped around the heavy shaft. He made his way to the back of the queue. In front of him they were almost all tourists, with their floppy hats, sandals and shorts. A few wore suits; business men (bastards) who were taking over the place as old buildings were demolished to make way for their new waterside apartments. He stood out from both groups, belonging to neither, with his grubby t-shirt and grease-soiled jeans. He joined them, waiting in the early morning sunshine, not worried about the showers that were blowing from the east. He wasn't worried about rain. The tourists will have their day spoiled, and that gave him a little satisfaction. The short ferry ride would take them across to Valletta. The waterfront was jammed with ostentatious yachts, reflecting their ostentatious wealth in the warm Mediterranean. Bastards!

BALCONIES

The Akvarium chugged alongside the jetty, and the ticket collector jumped ahead of the queue of departing passengers to set up his tiny booth, and took the fares as they all clambered aboard. The tourists were noisy, excited. The businessmen were solemn, serious. He felt in his pocket for the two euro coins and handed them across the makeshift counter. In return he was passed a ticket. Within a few minutes the ferry was on its way, zigzagging across to the stops that lined the harbour side on its way through the creek. Then suddenly they would be out into the choppier water of the Grand Harbour before moving onto Valletta itself, the high forbidding city walls looming above them as they drew near. There were plenty of empty seats - it was still too early for all but the most dedicated tourists - but he stood at the bow, watching the grand arches and stone battlements of the Three Cities pass, chugging to the ferry terminus way below the cannons that stood in The Barrakka Gardens. Adrian stood still, and waited, eyes forward, fingers caressing the screwdriver, thinking only of his task. All around him cameras clicked and gasps of *oohs* and *aahs* formed a background hum as they passed the yachts, each bigger than a house. Their flags fluttered in the breeze that would bring the rain; flags that betrayed the origin of their owners: Scandinavian, Russian, British, Italian, French. A United Nations on water. Dust was everywhere in the background, making the sunshine hazy. Soon the whole place would be changed to make way for the

BALCONIES

uber-rich and their super-yachts. "Bastards!" he muttered, not quite soft enough to be unheard.

Adrian had ridden this ferry so many times. It held no wonders for him. Instead he allowed his mind to wander back to earlier that morning: the ping of his phone - old but still 'smart' enough - that signalled the arrival of her instructions. The details were clear enough; a straightforward job. He had sent no reply, asked no questions. And the final order: *Obey instructions to the letter, and the money will follow…*

Once the ferry had docked it was just a matter of crossing the road and getting into the elevator, slipping through the control gate without need of a ticket. In another hour it would be impossible, but the fat controller, in his quasi-military uniform, hadn't started his shift yet. There was no-one to recognise him if the need ever arose, if the police… The lift carried him rapidly, high above the dockside, almost sickeningly rapid. The view over the water was what the tourists loved, but he barely noticed it, waiting impatiently for the doors to slide open. He made his way, pushing against the throng, through the gardens and onward towards the bus station. He was on the bus before the rain came. It was a shower. It would not last long.

The number twelve bus wove its way along the coastline, past rocky inlets and busy Paceville, where last night's revellers were returning to the waterside bars to top up their alcohol levels. The bus journey was tedious but at this time they ran from the city centre almost empty. Adrian sat staring,

BALCONIES

unseeing, the screwdriver still clutched in his hand. He longed for the big pay-day when he could dispense with the bus rides and run his own BMW, or better still on his car-crammed rock, afford to take taxis wherever he went.

It had all started with that first phone call, six months ago. She had known he was broke, desperate. The job had been simple enough, disabling the CCTV cameras at the hotel, *"just long enough"*, she'd said without saying for what. Wearing a cap, carrying a screwdriver, these were the things that made him invisible in a large hotel. He had even had a nod from one of the elaborately-dressed men at the desk, as though in recognition. Then nothing from her until this morning; he'd waited impatiently for the pay-day. It had taken a long time but now it was close. After this it was all over and the money would be on its way. Easy money she had promised, and easy money it had been - except for the waiting, that hadn't been easy.

The bus stopped for a while on the Mosta Road; the rain was being swept aside from the windscreen. The driver said something about a car crash, but Adrian took no notice. Another tourist driving too fast on slick roads, no doubt. The bus continued on its way to Bugibba Harbour. The rain was gone. He stepped down into the hot sunshine, took out his phone and looked at the screen. Not quite ten o'clock. It was

BALCONIES

nearly time. He glanced up at the block above him, feigning indifference, taking in the detail of the second-floor balcony. He turned his back on it and looked out to sea, beyond the harbour wall, watching tourists jostle past each other to be first on the boat that waited there. Another bus arrived at the stop. He resisted the pull to see who disembarked, continuing to watch the bobbing boats. A klaxon sounded; a gangplank was lifted; it was time. Adrian turned and saw the man leaving the building. Slowly he climbed the hill that wove its way past the little chapel. The door was ajar, just as she'd said. He pulled it shut behind him, hearing the latch engage. He shunned the lift and made his way up the stairs, two at a time. The screwdriver was out of his pocket now and in his hand. The job was as good as done. Then he'd show those bastards…

BALCONIES

FIVE

THE GO-BETWEEN, KALKARRA

Valery watches the balcony.
It has been a busy morning. But there is still more to do. First he'd gone to Il-Mdina to leave the car, the keys accessible, the note on the wheel. The night before he'd left his own car in a side street in Rabat, so it was a quick transfer and drive to Bugibba Square. He suspected that the package in the boot was a gun, but he hadn't asked her. It was best to listen. Then, with the new package (money, perhaps) in his pocket, he walked on to the harbour wall at St. Paul's Bay. From here he can see the apartment, the balcony open. He sees the man

BALCONIES

leave through the front door, pulling it closed behind him, the screwdriver still in his hand. He thinks he detected a smile on the engineer's face.

Valery too had smiled earlier, standing on his balcony overlooking the still, grey sea. Today it will be all over and he will leave this island at last; and not on his own. Her husband was dead, and now he would take his place alongside her. They would start a new life together, "Somewhere in Italy," she'd said, giving no more clues, "with a whole bundle of money". He looks again at the apartment block door. Nothing to report. The engineer has done his job; all was going to plan. He watches him as he drops downhill then out of sight. The next time he would see him they would be in Valletta. He looks at his watch, and begins his slow walk back to the car. The rain has stopped. There is time, plenty of time, before he would see him again. As he climbs back into the car, the radio gives out the news he'd been expecting: *Fatality; a blue Peugeot car; out of control; crossed the roundabout; crashed through a wall; hurtling down the side of the hill.* He has expected it, waiting for it, but even so it comes as a shock. He turns the radio off, not wanting to hear any more. He eases his foot off the accelerator. Instinctive; something we all do when we hear of another's misfortune. Except racing drivers, apparently, or that's what he'd read somewhere. He imagines the scene at the bottom of the Victoria Lines, the balcony of a wall that the British had built

BALCONIES

some time last century to fend off attacks. Ah yes, the British. They were to blame for all of Malta's troubles, and much of Europe too. He hated the British, with their *jolly old pals* act. The British who sauntered round the island as though they still owned it. Piece by piece it is being bought up by his people, Russians, who would soon be in control. Perhaps they would even change the rules of the road - driving on the left! He moves the car into the left-hand lane and turns towards Valletta. He passes a bus with its crowd of passengers heading for the capital; perhaps one of them was the man he'd spoken to earlier ; the man with the gun - for he was certain it was a gun. He has to be there before him; needs a good viewpoint at the Gardens, so that he won't be recognised and to be sure all goes according to plan. As she had arranged. He thinks of her again, and he feels the smile returning to his face. He licks his lips greedily: the woman and the money! Answering her advert was the best move he'd ever made. It is the best job, and the easiest money, he will ever earn. And the woman? Keep your mind on the job. One foot in front of the other. There will be time for such thoughts later. Osel! Donkey! One step at a time. She is the real prize. Don't blow it, Valery, you donkey. His father always called him that. *You always get ahead of yourself, donkey. Take it slow and steady. One step at a time.* Although he hadn't thought so then, his father had given him good advice.

BALCONIES

Traffic into Valletta is virtually at a standstill. It always is. The rain that had started when he was in Mdina had washed downhill and gathered at the waterside in Gzira and cars and buses slipped and splashed along the puddled roads throwing plumes of water onto unsuspecting pedestrians. The blue-black sheen of the tarmac gives the appearance of a mirror, reflecting the sky in a shimmering haze. One mistake here will result in a lengthy delay, or worse - he smiles at the irony. So he puts the music on the radio. He is ahead of the bus and the time is still good. The lights change twice more before he pulls away, alongside the creek filled with launches and yachts - perhaps he'll have a boat of his own soon. Why not? The road swings up the hill, and through the ornate arched gates that herald the city centre. He parks the car, paying the man with the claw fingers and wonky hips, the two euros. It's already twenty minutes to twelve.

"Grazzi," he says, and pockets the coin. "Grazzi", as though it's a small fortune. Then up the hill he goes, past the Phoenician Hotel and across the bridge. The lift entrance comes into view and he thinks again of the pieces that must come together. Two men, and a gun. By noon. High Noon. The noon gun! He smiles. If only they knew.

The noon gun. Paul looks at his watch and drums his fingers impatiently on the metal rail that stands above the courtyard where the cannons sit, pointing across the harbour ready to

BALCONIES

fire their noon blast for the tourists. He feels into his back pocket, reaches for the picture once again and looks hard into the eyes of his prey. He can see why she has chosen this time and place. As noon approaches it gets even busier.

Adrian has his hands in his pocket, rubbing his calloused fingers along the point of the screwdriver. He looks around, recalling the message. *Meet me at the balcony at Barrakka Gardens. Wait for me there, at the front of the balcony.* He can see why she has chosen this time and place. It is busy, and getting busier as noon approaches.

Valery watches them both, from his viewpoint, behind the pillar. He can see why she has chosen this time and place. It is teeming with tourists as the final act approaches. The shooter is to his right, the engineer to his left, and at the bottom of the hill below Mtarfa, the chauffeur lies dead. Yes, it is all going to plan. It had been the work of only a moment to slice through the brake cables. Of course there had been a patch of fluid beneath the car, but then he'd pushed it to another space before parking it. Unnecessary, as it turned out. The rain will have washed away all evidence. His watch shows the two hands closing together. The shooter is getting close to the rail. Valery can see the shape of the gun in his pocket - but then he knows it's there. The engineer leans forward over the rail, looking down onto the cannons below, for all the world a

BALCONIES

tourist waiting for the action to start. Valery looks at the scene playing out ahead of him.

The actor-soldier on the gun-terrace below is finishing his speech. The other, dressed alike in a nineteenth-century military uniform, positions himself alongside the cannon. The blast when it comes, just a nano-second after the flash, draws a gasp from the crowd, as it always does. and then, once the echo dies, a round of applause. None of them notice the man slumped over the rail, his hand still in his pocket, wrapped around the screwdriver. Those who perhaps favour him with more than a glance are already on their way. There are other sights to see, lunches to be enjoyed. Neither do they pay any heed to the man pushing his way past them, back into the gardens, back towards the bus station. He is in a hurry. There is a pile of money awaiting him in an apartment in St. Paul's Bay. Only Valery notices them both, and knows how well-timed the single shot has been. The shooter is an artist! Two were dead. The Russian moves through the crowd, following briefly the same direction as Paul, but then he breaks off and returns to the car park. He sits at the wheel, watches the attendant who is busy with new arrivals, his twisted fingers and crooked hip. Life will be different now for him, Valery. With money in his pocket and a beautiful woman on his arm, he is ready for a new life in Sicily, for it is there that they will go, he is sure. His father would at last be proud of him, what he has made of himself. He is someone, now.

BALCONIES

The bus is full. Paul has managed to get himself to the front of the queue. The barrel of the gun feels hot against his chest, but he smiles at how well he had done. An artist at work. Perfect timing. One shot - one clap of a cannon - perfectly synchronised. He had rehearsed it in his head all the way, and now he can marvel at the smoothness of it all. She had been adamant: *one more job and it will all be over.* And he'll be very rich. Four was now three so his share will have grown. He has taken all the risk so that is how it should be. Just a final trip back to the apartment where he will collect the money. Then it really will be all over. He has already booked a room at an expensive hotel, and tomorrow he will pay the money into his bank account and see a man about an apartment. Something flashy. Soon he'd be 'home and hosed', ready for the next adventure. But not with her. He is done with her. Now he would work for himself. He is a winner. The journey seems to be taking forever. The bus's air conditioning blasts out cold air but he still feels sticky and his shirt sticks to him. He keeps his hand across his chest, hiding the gun's profile. When he gets back to the bay, the gun will go into the sea. It is deep enough to lie there unseen. No-one will ever find it, and in any case there will be no link to him.

Valery heads back to Kalkarra, the last act still to be played out. It is a Russian drama with a Mediterranean setting.

BALCONIES

Tolstoy and Shakespeare plotting together for the perfect scenario. The parking space is still free; he reverses into it, turns the key and sits with the radio on. So far the death of the man from Birgu has not been mentioned, but it is only a matter of time. By then he, Valety, and she, The Woman, will be on their way out of Malta, across the sea, north to Sicily. She had shown him the pictures of the pretty village with its balcony overlooking the bay. He switches off the radio, opens the door and slides out, slamming it shut behind him. He looks up at the balcony. He will miss Kalkarra, but he is moving to something much better.

Paul turns his key and steps onto the balcony overlooking St. Paul's Bay. He loves this view, the sea so close you can almost touch it. He wants a last look. How predictable he is. This view is so inviting, and he never tires of it. He moves closer to the balcony and leans against it as he watches two cats climb out of the shrubbery below…

BALCONIES

SIX

THE WOMAN, SICILY

Three unrelated incidents:
A tourist falls from a balcony;
A local man is shot in Valletta;
A car accident.

So tragic.
She looks out again at the white parasols lined up alongside the Mediterranean. Perhaps she will miss these people; they have

BALCONIES

been so kind: the porters, the maids, the waiters. Even the police.

We're so sorry about your husband. A terrible business. And you must have been terrified... She had to admit, yes, she had been afraid, just a little. But she had not needed to be; things had gone exactly as planned. They had believed her story, told with tears and sobs. And now, with it all behind her, she could leave this island once and for all and join her lover in Sicily. She looks again at the screen, at the message, and closes the lid of her computer. She turns instead to the mirror and takes another look at her makeup and hair. Tomorrow morning will be her last in Malta. She will take the ferry, joining the others, mainly one-day tourists, across the straits to her island of dreams, with its pretty seaside villages, perched high on the cliffs, and its brooding volcano with grey powdery sides. Volcanoes suit her, matching her personality. All that heat below the surface, waiting to erupt. Just one more job to do. She returns to the bedroom and goes through the drawers carefully. No trace of her must be left here; her departure must be complete, entire. The drawers are empty. In the bathroom, there are just those few things she will need for her early morning departure. She picks up the phone, dials zero,

BALCONIES

and waits. The voice at the other end is as smooth and unhurried as she has tried to make her own.

"I just want to confirm that the early morning taxi is booked…"

"Yes, madam, for six o'clock, as you requested. Have no fear, madam. It will be here on time."

"Thank you," she says and she hears her own smooth rolling tones disappear down the line, charming and cajoling as ever. She has practised this voice, this look, this whole persona, and she will miss it when she leaves Malta. She will miss the power it has given her over others - especially gullible men! She returns the phone to its cradle and looks at her nails. Russian men seem to like their women with auburn hair and blood-red nails, and she wants Valery to like her.

She returns to the balcony and sits on the white plastic chair, overlooking the bay. To her left, the glass modernity of Sliema; to her right, the imposing stone walls of Valletta. For all its claustrophobia, she has enjoyed her brief stay here; has marvelled at the people and its history. She hadn't thought she would. Malta had been her husband's choice; as usual she had gone along with him, but she was a free woman. Now that he is gone from her life, she will always think of Malta as a

BALCONIES

special place! But she will not return, just in case. The money from her husband's emptied account is all safely packed in the case - she cannot resist turning back to look at it once again, in one bundle now, but with room in the bag for a little more. Consolidation. She feels no remorse. It is her due. That miserly, miserable husband of hers had kept her on a tight leash all these years, spending money that should have been hers on his mistress. And all the while keeping her on a budget, and in his power. Well, he is dead, and she will not mourn his loss, despite the open show of grief she has shown. All part of the act. If she *had* loved him, she might be thinking of revenge on the mistress who'd spent *her* money, but she will suffer enough now that the spring was dry, now that the well and not just her bed was empty. The greedy bitch will have to go elsewhere for her sugar. No. Revenge was not necessary. She has all the satisfaction she needs.

As for those men, they were geedy. They gave no thought to each other; they were happy to increase their own pile. Now they have paid the price. And tomorrow she will have *him* back in her arms. He adores her, she knows that, and together, in Sicily, they can make a good life for themselves. She takes a last look over the balcony at the bare chests and

BALCONIES

bikinis that lie frying in the late afternoon sunshine, then turns away, setting off to the dining room for a last supper. Then, when she returns to her room, there will be plenty to do before the morning.

At six o'clock the limousine pulls up alongside the hotel entrance. The driver sits still, behind the wheel, while the concierge opens the boot, loads the three matching suitcases and closes it with a slam.
"Come back to us again, madam, in better circumstances," adds the concierge as he closes the door behind her with another slam. The driver is sorely tempted to protest to the concierge but refrains. The woman who climbs in the back is clearly used to good service and the driver smells a big tip. He bites his tongue again. Why do they have to slam doors? This is a limousine. It needs more gentle handling - like the woman herself. He looks at her in the mirror, letting his eyes linger longer than strictly necessary. She sees him and smiles, her tongue between her teeth.
 "The ferry port, madam?"
No answer.
"You are off to Sicily?"

BALCONIES

No answer, but this time he sees her smile. She looks even more beautiful when she smiles.

"Is it just a day trip?"

No answer again, but her smile broadens - wide enough to break his heart. And he smiles too as he pulls out of the hotel drive and turns downhill for the five minute drive. He smiles at the anticipation of a large tip.

She waits in line, her head covered by a pretty shawl. In all other ways she is undistinguished, undistinguishable. She is, to all eyes, just another day-tripper who fills the boat all year round. Her luggage has already been taken from her, and sent on board. In that sense she *is* different from her fellow-travellers. Few of them have luggage, merely the on-board bags crammed to bursting with cameras, phones, tourist leaflets and euros. She hands over her passport to the woman, with the ticket tucked inside. To the official's eyes, she is cool, she is calm, she is collected. Only she herself can feel the racing heartbeat. She has seen him, Valery, lining up ahead of her. *Make no contact. We'll meet in the bar on board... Two strangers enjoying an early morning coffee.*

BALCONIES

"Good morning, madam." The woman in a dark blue skirt and light blue shirt looks straight at her. Does she know? Is she about to be discovered? Will they stop her? She stares straight back at the woman in blue, who looks again at the passport photo, smiles and tears the ticket in half. Then she returns the passport with what remains of the ticket.

"Buon viaggio, signora. Enjoy Sicily"

"I għandu. Grazzi." And she is waved through. A huge sigh escapes her whole body. She makes her way onto the boat, keeping her eyes downcast. It will not do for too many people to see her. Just another Maltese woman off on a day trip. Most of the seats in the central aisle are still empty as people flock to the window seats to get the best views of their journey. Children, barely awake, are already bored and impatient to know: *are we nearly there yet?* even before the ferry has departed. She ignores them all, glances up at the screen, where she sees images of her beloved Sicily - of sea, and sand and flower-decked balconies in those pretty hilltop villages. And of Mount Etna, smoking, above it all. There is a magazine in the seat back and she opens it, looking fondly at the glossy images, imagining herself as their subject, adorning those pages. Not right away of course. It will be unseemly to

BALCONIES

be seen spending her money so soon after her husband's murder. From all she knows about Sicily, few will take notice of the mysterious couple living in their seaside villa. In Sicily it doesn't pay to ask too many questions. Many people have discovered that! She glances across towards the bar. A few men have settled onto high stools, already drinking sweet thick espressos. There is no sign of Valery, but it is early yet. The ferry has still not left Valletta.

Valery spots her, seated alone, next to the aisle. He pats his pocket as he passes - the money still wrapped in the same bundle. Her bag occupies the seat next to her, and alongside a family of three, with the small boy watching the television screen, his eyes wide, his thumb jammed into his mouth. The shawl hides her hair, her beautiful red hair, but he remembers its length, its curl and its colour, and longs to see her shake it free, next to him. Valery must be patient! He tries to catch her eye - just a stranger ogling a pretty woman. She, for her part, keeps her eyes glued to the magazine, though he knows she has seen him. There is a smile playing on her lips. He sits on a seat three rows behind her. He looks at his watch. Was it only yesterday…? And now, here they both are,

BALCONIES

Sicily-bound, with a wonderful life mapped out for them. She had shown him pictures of the villa, with its balcony high above the Mediterranean. The boat is on its way. He is on his way. They are on their way.

The Malta coastline is far behind them, passing St. Paul's Bay far away over to the port side. He hadn't waited to see the final act, but now he imagines the shooter, plummeting streetward as the loosened balcony gave way... *Not enough regulation...Ministers will look into tightening up building regulations... New legislation...*

He swings his legs into the aisle, stands and goes to the bar. There he sits on one of the last two stools left vacant, and even though he looks straight ahead at the barman, he knows she has taken the stool next to him.

"A coffee please. Cappuccino." The barman slips a saucer in front of him, adds spoon and sugar lumps, and then the coffee cup, still hot and frothing. He puts the five euro note down in front of him and the barman leaves the change in a neat pile.

"Americano, please." He hears her voice, and feels his spine tingle at the sound of it, as it always does. At last they will be together. He has done everything she has asked to free him of the husband. She will know how to reward him. At last they will be together, and rich. Very rich. Her coffee comes and

BALCONIES

she sips at it. The barman goes across to serve another customer at a table, but Valery notices how his eyes stay on her. Valery unwraps the sugar and drops two lumps through the froth into the thick dark mixture. All the time, his eyes look at the cup, straining to resist the urge to look at her. He smells the coffee, mingling with the smell of her perfume. What is it? He will learn soon enough. He will know everything about her. She drops a coin as she fumbles the change into her purse, and it rolls down into the body of the bar. The barman picks it up mid-roll, and stands with it in his hand. He is unsure who has dropped it. Valery smiles at her, goes across to the barman and takes the coin. He places it on the bar in front of her. He never once looks at her. He is afraid he will give himself away. They are strangers; to all the world they are strangers.

"Yours, I think."

"Thank you." She takes the coin and then her cup, brushes past him as the boat rolls, then she returns to her seat alongside the aisle, retrieves her magazine and their meeting is over. And all the while Valery warms his fingers around the coffee cup.

The next time we meet will be at the villa. You have the directions? Good. I'll be there. Be patient.

BALCONIES

He remembers the instructions and he will follow them. Now is not the time for impatience. He hears his father's voice, as he always does when he is nervous and impatient. *Don't get ahead of yourself, donkey. One step at a time.*
He drinks the coffee, its warm, bitter taste filling his mouth. He leaves the bar, pats his pocket again. The package is still there. He returns to his seat with that slightly drunken roll induced by the moving boat. He sits down. It is still early morning and he feels tired. Such an early start after a long and busy yesterday. He closes his eyes.

She leaves the magazine on the seat beside her, joins the queue for disembarkation and waits patiently for her luggage and then her taxi. Her hand involuntarily moves to her left pocket where she feels the slip of paper, still creased into its shape, and the gritty remains of powder brush against her fingertips. She screws it up, takes it into her hand and drops it into the water as she crosses the gangplank into Sicily. She hears the police sirens as she collects her bags, loading them onto a trolley. Ready now, she wheels it to a waiting white-topped limousine.

BALCONIES

The driver greets her, but she says nothing. Instead she passes him the card with the address.

"Sì signora." And as the taxi starts to move away she sees the police car slow up alongside the walkway, and even before it has stopped, two officers running up onto the ferry.

"Drunken tourists," her driver says, touching his finger to his head.

"English! They make so much trouble!" She touches her hand to the package in her right coat pocket and feels the packet there. At last she is in Sicily. And Valery was dead.

Tony sits on the balcony, watching the sea roll onto the sandy beach. Geraniums shine bright red in the terracotta pots that hang from the balcony rail. Soon she will arrive and he will have her again. Only this time she will not have a husband; just his money. He hears a car in the street below. He stands and looks over the balcony. She smiles up at him, her hair dark brown and falling loosely about her shoulders. *I am in love.*

BALCONIES

Tenerife

Wherever she goes, dead bodies pile up. But her hands are clean.

The Woman has moved on to Tenerife where there is more cleaning-up to do.

Another thriller in six acts.

BALCONIES

The Waiter wants money - enough to start his own bar in Tenerife - and blackmail is the easiest way.

The Sweet Senorita wants excitement and is happy to be part of a drug sting.

The Security Guard wants a better life with an exotic woman. And The Woman? She just wants to be free of her past.

Four people thrown together on a holiday island; who will survive?

BALCONIES

ARRIVALS

The Giants: mighty rocks. Their feet stand fast and deep below the Atlantic Ocean; their heads soar high into the clouds towering above the breaking tide. They were born out of terrible pain and fire, and rose from upheavals beneath the sea. Here they stand, still and steady, defining the landscape, precipitous balconies over the bulldozing surf. Do they feel the urge to move, to stride across the water, to break free? They felt their mother's pain and still bear the scars of its cataclysm. They are giants in stature but they are a volcanic mother's children and she calls to them, urges them to take their first steps, like any child. These are the walls of hell, known to Guanche people long before the holidaymakers

BALCONIES

came. They have seen love, and they have seen death. And they are unmoved by both.

The plane banks, dipping its portside wing in a salute to her, the woman with her red lips and matching fingernails. She imagines its occupants. This is their first sight of the holiday island. In the cabin, hands grip just a little tighter onto arm-rests and jaws chew sweets just a little more resolutely; but not her hands and not her jaws. To her, flying presents no fears. There are worse ways to die. She knows about death. And she knows, also, about love. She watches its flight path as it makes its way past her balcony, and she returns the salute with a red-lipped smile. The plane has arrived.

The plane banks again, more steeply this time. He watches the descent, a little nervous. His palms are sweaty but his patience has been rewarded by the sight of the giant cliffs above the water and then, higher still, snow-tipped Teide, clouds wreathed about its mighty shoulders so it looks for all the world like a floating hill. The runway stretches out below and the pilot lines up for the final descent. Another set of holidaymakers are duly delivered, to replace those already set to depart back to colder, darker northern lands. The hushed nervous pause in the cabin gives way to clicks of belts and bright chatter as the 'can't wait to get off' crowd rummage around in the overhead lockers. The waiter sits, patient; no

BALCONIES

need for him to hurry. As the doors open the humid air fills the cabin, carrying with it promises of sunbeds, swimming pools and sinking cocktails on the balcony. The holiday season is in full swing.

Sicily is behind her now, a glorious past. From here on the balcony she can see the grey-blue waters of the Atlantic, and behind her stands the mountains. What is it about volcanoes that draw her so? Hot smoking giants that hide black secrets below: first Etna and now Teide. Perhaps they draw her because she has their nature. She frowns and the lines pull at her forehead as she remembers her beloved Sicily. This is a new country. There are new contracts to fulfil. She is tired of the constant travel. But this island of continuous summer will be just a temporary home. There is already a flight booked… She looks at her pocket mirror and resets her smile, pleased with what she sees. Blond hair and red lips. Appearances are everything. Men are easily fooled, taken in by outward show. It gives women power over men, and she would be as foolish as them to ignore it. On her balcony, high above the breaking Atlantic surf, she looks to where the plane has disappeared below the horizon. He has arrived. It is time. The brief holiday is over.

At the airport the young girl, Spanish black hair and eyes, watches the passengers as they pour through the arrivals gate.

BALCONIES

She looks at her phone again, at the picture displayed there, and waits impatiently for the match like a child's game of Duo. She sees him come, *long fair hair tied in a ponytail* – and resists the urge to shout "Snap". She watches as he picks up the backpack again and starts to rezip it, returning his passport to the pouch inside. She brushes past him just as she was told:
"Lo siento, señor. Perdóname."
He nods at her. He smiles at her, a sweet senorita. Sure, a pretty girl is always a pleasure. Her eyes follow him to the filing taxis. It was all easier than she had imagined. She watches him get in then calls the number she has been given and says what she has been told to say.
"El está aqui, Senora."

She takes the message without speaking.
She looks in the mirror again.
Good.
He has arrived.
Now it can end.

BALCONIES

ONE: The Waiter

My dad said I'll never amount to much. What he'd actually said was: "You're a useless idle shit who'll never make an honest living!" And maybe he was right. I'm always on the lookout for a dishonest one. But I haven't killed anyone – yet! And that's more than he can say. He was a joke, my dad. Known around the barracks as 'Lieutenant Col' – he was actually a lieutenant named Colin but he fancied himself and wore a chip on his shoulder, rather than a pip, feeling that he'd been overlooked for inferior men. I don't know whether he ever heard the joke – perhaps he himself put it about to assume

BALCONIES

greater importance; it was typical of the man. He was a bully and a cheat. Perhaps the thirty or so men in his charge adored him, but none of his family did.

When mum died a year after I'd walked out of my college A-Levels (English and Economics) he laid that at my door; but it was the cancer that killed her. That and life with a rotten husband. I was living in Streatham and working in a bar in Bermondsey for minimum wage and tips, taking on an Irish accent 'cos, sure, everyone loves the Irish don't they, and you get bigger tips. I went home to Windsor for the funeral. The coffin had been so small and light. The disease had eaten her from the inside so there was little left to bury.

"What will you do now, Robbie?" the aunts wanted to know. Mum's sisters had miraculously appeared having been invisible all her married life.

"You needn't think you're coming back here to live off me," was all he'd said. My dad, the war hero! The Irish accent was a double whammy: bigger tips, and it got right up his nose. He hated the Irish. Three years posting in Londonderry had only deepened the hate. It was all part of my divorce from him. I smiled and stuck two fingers up at him (out of reach of his fists of course) and we never spoke to each other again. That was two years ago.

Working in a bar suited me. I saw myself as a Lothario, chatting up the birds and pouring cocktails. Most of the staff

BALCONIES

were temping, filling in time on a gap year between A-Levels and Uni. But for me it was a career choice. I loved it. Home was wherever I ended up – rarely in my own bed-sit. Rarely in my own bed!

Then the chance came to follow the sun south. I spoke a little Italian (public school hadn't been a complete waste of money) and saw a job advertised on the ferries that ran between Malta and Sicily. It was a change from the wet dark winters and the wet dull summers of a London suburb so I jumped at it. I dropped the accent – sounding English was a real advantage in Malta so I reluctantly gave up the lilt. There was a plan – sure everyone has a plan? I wanted my own bar – Robbie's Irish bar – somewhere hot. Tenerife sounded just perfect. And now I was within touching distance. All the squirrelling away little bits of cash would never get me my dream, but now... It was my big chance.

I remember it clearly. The boat left Valletta early as usual. It was still dark when the first customers came to drink. She left her magazine on the seat and came to the bar for a coffee. There wasn't much call for cocktails before breakfast. The evening run was more fun. She ordered a coffee and even the way she drank it – with those full lips – oozed sex and wealth. Her head was covered in a silk scarf, expensive, and wisps of deep auburn hair escaped to soften and frame her face. She was older than she looked but I was up for it... I was happy to be her toy boy (is that phrase still used?). She could finance

BALCONIES

my project – a sugar mommy. Why not? Then the Russian came. He was acting coy as if he didn't know her but you can't kid a kidder. They were an item all right. So I gave her up as a lost job and set my sights on a young Italian in a very skimpy skirt. But I saw her – madam silk scarf – I saw her. She took a powder from her sleeve like some magician and poured it into his drink while he followed a rolling coin. Then she was gone. It was only when the police came on board and started asking questions that I gave it any more thought.
"I don't remember anything at all about the man who died" was all I'd said. I wasn't above a bit of blackmail. A dream is a dream and this dream was being given life by a streak of good fortune – luck of the Irish I call it. I saw her again in one of the Italian papers left on the boat at the end of another Sicily day-trip. And there was her picture on the front page mourning the loss of her Italian lover. Oh the hair was down and the lips were red but there was no mistaking her. Three days later I had the address and I wrote the letter. Then on one of my trips to Sicily I went AWOL and sought her out. That meeting was the beginning of my new life.

There's a man begging outside the gates. I've been waiting for handouts too. You get nowhere like that.
"Get yourself a job, mate…"
I take the lift to the top floor. The Gigansol is a twelve storey palace of an apartment block. From the balcony the pool

BALCONIES

sparkles blue and gold, reflecting the bright sunshine in the cloudless sky. It's very warm and my shirt is sticking to my back. The airport transfer was a hot sweaty cab ride.

"This is just the sort of place I want," I'd told the agent on the phone. "I've come into some money. My mother's just died and I have an inheritance." Half-truths were always best. The picture on the website sold it to me. "Any chance of booking it for a week to see how I like it?" He'd been happy with the idea. It was empty and it was a commission. He was a fellow traveller making some money for *his* dream. The owners had put it up for sale and gone back to England. They were desperate.

"Brexit!" was all the agent had said. "Difficult times for you Brits."

"I'm Irish," I'd lied – some real blarney! So now, here I am at the Gigansol - between a rock and a Lidl, in the heart of Los Gigantes with views over the sea and a bright blue pool. And all around me are bars with 'Se Vende' signs. I stand on the balcony, leaning my weight on my elbows, watching the bathers below, looking for girls alone, or better still, girls in pairs. Sure what's the harm in it? There's no-one at home waiting for me. There are three together in skimpy bikinis. You can't have too much of a good thing. From here they look good, but I need to get down there and work some magic. First though I need to unpack my bag. There isn't much. I don't accumulate. I undo the zip, and there on top is an envelope. Not mine -

BALCONIES

brown manila, small. And inside? A portable phone. How did it get in here, I wonder? This is her doing! I look at it — cheap, the sort you buy for calls only when you're abroad. It starts to vibrate in my hand.

BALCONIES

TWO: La Senorita

"No. I need to see your boarding card." My English isn't perfect but surely this stupid woman understands. "Not your passport, senora, er madame. Your boarding card." This time she gets it; flashes the folded paper at me. I take the number of her flight and press the keys of the computerised till. "Thank you, madam. Have a good flight." She smiles and I smile, knowing it is automatic. I am invisible. I am just another airport worker. To her and to all the others maybe, but today I am an undercover cop.

BALCONIES

I met Mario for the first time yesterday evening – is that his real name I wonder? Is he undercover too? - moments before the end of my shift. It had been just another day at the store, smiling sweetly and spraying perfume onto veined and bony wrists. He wore dark pants and a pale blue shirt with the badge: *Security Officer*. He was younger than most of them. Good body and black hair. He told me:
"We've been watching you senorita." I saw him glance at my ring finger.
"Watching me?" I was coming to the end of my probationary month so I feared the next sentence. I couldn't afford to lose this job yet. "Have I done something wrong?" Had it been that mix-up with the change yesterday evening? *That wasn't my fault,* I was about to say. *The man...* But he smiled. At least his mouth did. I couldn't see his eyes behind the pilots. But I bet they were deep brown.
"We want you to do some work for us."
"For us?"
"Security." He spoke Spanish with a Catalan accent. It was a warm sound to my Barcelona ears. All of the airport workers had accents of one type or another, so it was nice to hear his familiar sound.
"Security? But I'm just a student."
"We know all about you, senorita."
And then he told me all about the sting that was being set up for the English boy coming in on the next flight.

BALCONIES

"He's carrying drugs – to distribute here at the clubs on the Playa Americas." He sent a picture of the boy: long fair hair tied back in a short ponytail. Take your break so that you can see him arrive. Then get this envelope into his backpack somehow."

"How will I do that?"

"You're a bright girl – law degree isn't it? – you'll think of something."

Part of me was so excited. Here I was taking part in a drugs bust – is that the term? But:

"Why me?"

"He won't be suspicious of a young Spanish girl in a 'Tenerife Duty Free' blouse. With a sweet senorita smile."

"What if I get caught?"

"We'll be on hand. But don't get caught. The team here has put a lot of hours into setting this up..." And he smiled again.

"Yes, sir. I do need to see your boarding card - Ihre Bordkarte. For the duty free it's necessary. Notwendig!" The elderly German frowns at me and puts his bag down in a manner that shows he is thoroughly pissed off. But I smile my *sweet senorita smile* and he emerges with it. I note the number, wrap his bottle of schnapps, hand it to him and take his euros. "Thank you, sir, have a nice day. Guten Tag." And as he turns away my face returns to its natural shape. Smiling all day at stupid tourists is hard work, let me tell you. The boy

BALCONIES

has been and gone. Getting the envelope in his bag was easier than I'd imagined. He looked like a sweet boy. But these days you can't tell a drug smuggler from a German shopper. The whole thing had lasted a matter of seconds. But I had been so nervous, sweat above my lips and on my back. The security officer comes back at the end of my shift. To all the world he is just chatting me up:
"And..."
"Just like you said. It was simple."
"Well done senorita," in his familiar Catalan. He hands me an envelope, and at first I think it is the same one I dropped into the boy's luggage, but this is lighter. I can feel the outline of a locker key inside it: a packet of euros in a deposit box somewhere? And he is gone again, into the crowd. Perhaps I should have asked for a payment now. Why not? It's obviously worth something to foil a big drugs gang, and some euros in my pocket tonight... Still it was worth it. Wait till I tell the girls on my course.

I remembered his words: "Keep it quiet, senorina. No-one must know about it. Until we have him behind bars. Then we'll give you your thousand euros, and you can tell all your friends."

No, I'd better wait. Sara and Mariana will be *so* jealous. But a thousand euros will pay for next term with plenty to spare.

BALCONIES

It is already the end of February and the second semester will begin soon. Law studies back in Barcelona will be so boring by comparison. When I'd told my parents I was spending the Christmas vacation in the airport shop in Tenerife they were horrified. Especially daddy.
"Is that what we're paying for?"
"I can earn some money and enjoy the sunshine. I can earn enough to pay for next term." Even mummy was sceptical:
"But what about your studies?"
They'd finally understood that we think differently from them, and in the end:
"Daddy's booked you a nice apartment away from Las Americas and all those druggies," mummy said. The whole of the rest of the world was dangerous in their eyes. "In Puerto Santiago. A nice place. Near the beach."
"It's all paid for – a month...."
"But," I'd complained. "It's much further from the airport. Can you imagine those bus rides every day?" I'd been fishing and caught a big one...
"We'll give you enough for taxis!" And so it had fallen into place. And they were right. It was a lovely apartment; small and bright with the afternoon sun on the balcony, for the odd days when I could enjoy it, overlooking Playa Arena. Reading law books in the warm winter sunshine on a terrace overlooking the sea is better than what the others would be doing. And I had a regular driver who picked me up at 7.40

BALCONIES

every work morning and gave me a cup of coffee to drink from a McDonald's cup. And here he is tonight at five o'clock waiting to take me back, with another coffee and a big smile.
"For my special senorita," he says and his gold tooth shines in the sunlight.
As I climb the stairs to my apartment my mobile vibrates in my bag...

BALCONIES

THREE: The Security Guard

By noon the air is hot. Only the cooling breeze makes the uniform wearable, bearable. I'm not used to wearing a uniform; uniforms – especially this uniform – are what I'd fought against all my life. When I decided to play the part, I remembered my father's uniform hanging in the hallway with its badged cap and epaulettes. He'd been nothing more than an airport shopping mall security guard from boyhood to his death, but he wore it like an army suit. Now I wear it as fancy-dress, to play a part, to win a prize. And what a prize! She is worth the winning,

BALCONIES

with her blond hair and bright red lips, and those eyes... To play a few games and win such a prize is every man's dream.

"Just a simple job. She's a young girl, on holiday, on her own. She'll fall for it: bring some excitement to her life, Mateo," and she'd flashed those beautiful eyes and pursed those blood-red lips. "And I'll bring some excitement to yours..." Her English was perfect, with a trace of Italian perhaps, which made her sound even more exotic. "When this is done, we can spend time together, here on your beautiful island."
It had all been straightforward. Wearing my father's uniform I would persuade the girl in the duty-free shop to drop a key into the boy's bag. She was part of a sting, and he was nothing more than a scumbag, blackmailing a beautiful woman because she needed to get rid of this unwanted Russian bully, who had followed her across Europe. She'd put a stop to him, but now this English boy was looking to line his pockets. Well that was something that I couldn't allow. The English boy must be made to see that he couldn't blackmail poor desperate women. The girl was – just as *she*'d suggested – flattered by the proposal, and had willingly done the job. Now, for the next twenty-four hours our lives are bound together, the four of us in a strange dance.

The walk from Puerto Santiago to Los Gigantes is short but all uphill. I glance up at the *sweet senorita*'s apartment above me

BALCONIES

as I pass. How can a student afford one of those luxury places while I live in my poky little place sharing a bathroom with God knows who and their shit? Not any more. I shall move in with my goddess. She has promised, and she will keep her promise. And before I go I'll have my revenge on those Russians in the flats with their not so carefully hidden stashes to sell on the Las Americas strip. These new mafia barons: they're going to pay for my new life. In the uniform, in the sunshine, it is a hard climb, but I stop on the balcony above the port, looking down at the tiny beach with its black volcanic grit, and straw sun shades like giant stick-men wearing sombreros. The diving board set above the rocky pool reflects the sun, but it is empty today. There are no divers here, only drinkers. The holiday makers in the bar below, men in shorts and ladies in bikinis, are drinking cerveza and rioja. I envy them their cool dress and tug at the shirt that sticks to my back. Another glance down at the surf breaking over black belligerent boulders before I make my way towards the tall grey apartment block

It was just over a month ago when I first saw her. Or rather she saw me... I spent most of my time back then on the open plaza at Arena, just down the road from my tiny apartment – I think flat's a better word; it's too small to be an apartment! I was sitting on the wall facing the sea. I think I was genuinely contemplating ending it all – this life on the island where I was

BALCONIES

born and which held no future for me. She must have read my thoughts.

"I hope you're not thinking of jumping," she'd said and the first thing I noticed was her red lips. "If you do, I should have to jump in and it will make a mess of my hair." She shook her head and that hair, a golden halo against the sun, framed her face. She was a goddess, an angel, my saviour.

"I am contemplating my future," I'd said.

"I'm glad you're thinking of having one. For a moment there I thought that perhaps..." and then she'd removed her shades and her face came alive with those blue eyes.

"I think I shall go to Spain, and try to find some work there. My mother was from Gerona and I still have cousins in Barcelona who will give me somewhere to sleep until I find somewhere of my own. Since my parents died there is little to keep me here." And she'd taken my arm, and back in her villa on the rocks above the bay she'd given me plenty of good reasons to stay. Afterwards, as we lay on the bed together, she told me about the waiter and the problems he was causing.

"All I want is to live my life, but I seem to attract men who want to do me harm, to cause me pain." And her voice broke and she cried in my arms. "I lost my beloved Tony to a heart attack. I thought we would build a life together. And if that wasn't enough this greedy boy comes along..."

And so we hatched the plan together. That night she sent the English waiter a brief text.

BALCONIES

"I'll pay you what you ask. But you must come here – to Tenerife to collect it. Then you will leave me alone."
I can't remember who suggested we use the girl.
"Yes. We need a sweet senorita," she had said with a smile. I told her about my dad's uniform folded up in the single box that remained of their possessions I'd taken from my parents' house. I could play the role of security guard at the airport and get someone innocent to do the drop.
She hadn't wanted to involve anyone else: "No-one must know, Mateo. I cannot take a risk that I will end up with another greedy bloodsucker..."
"Trust me," and I'd held her tighter. "There will be no-one to bother you; no-one to bother us."
"Flatter her and excite with promises of spying and perhaps a thousand euros, when the boy is gone." And it had all gone as planned.

Outside the tall grey apartment block I lean on the railing and watch more of them in the swimming pool. Is he there, amongst them, our little English blackmailer? There are three bikini-clad twenty-somethings sitting on the edge of the pool. I lean against the railings, an extinguished cigarette in my mouth, my hat pulled down over my brows, the heavy bag hidden beneath me, and a hand outstretched. He passes and mutters something under his breath. I spit on the floor as he passes. I imagine his journey up to the top floor.

BALCONIES

That's a long way to dive, is all I can think. Then the phone vibrates and I read the message.

BALCONIES

FOUR: The Woman

History constantly repeats itself. Déjà-vu is not just a feeling; it's a reality. There is nothing I won't do to re-capture that sense of wellbeing, of being safe. I thought I should never care for another life after my beloved Tony died. *A heart attack* the doctor had said, there in the apartment overlooking the sea at Taormina. *He had a weak heart.* Yes, I'd told him, but a very big one. And my tears had flowed, the first since those days of agony married to that monster in Malta. I hadn't wanted to leave Sicily, my adored Sicily, but it had been too hard to bear after Tony died. Poor Tony, I miss him. I had killed for him, and I had loved him. Perhaps there would be time for a new love when all this was done. Beloved Tony had lived barely

BALCONIES

three months after my journey to Taormina. I feel cheated of the life I had earned, the future I was promised.

The Russian's death was supposed to have ended it. I had been careless. Waiters are invisible and I hadn't seen him. Moving here to Tenerife is a temporary measure. I couldn't bear to see his things around me while my man himself is buried beneath the rich Sicilian soil. And then the wretched letter arrived. The local paper had taken pictures at the funeral – my beloved was loved by everybody and the church of the Madonna was filled. I clipped the article from the paper and then the English boy's letter arrived with the same picture and my face circled.

"Do you remember me?" his letter had asked. Of course I hadn't remembered him – who notices bar staff on a ferry boat? I had been careless, but there will be no more mistakes. I will use the gifts God has given me to finish the business once and for all. Men think they have all the power but I will show them all.

"The Russian was a bully," I had told him when he turned up at the apartment in Taormina. I was packing boxes ready to leave. And I described the way my dead husband had treated me only I attributed his cruelty to the Russian. "He was threatening me and I had to find a way to leave him." I watched him as I dabbed my eyes. As a child, crying had always come easily to me. And I watched him in my compact

BALCONIES

mirror as I touched up the red lipstick I keep especially for these occasions.

This move to Tenerife was quickly done. I took the green house on a six month lease, overlooking the sea in the resort of La Arena. I wasn't intending to stay that long. Behind me rose the high peak of Teide, snow-covered for much of the year; in front the sea, beating against the rocks on which the house stood and throwing spray onto the balcony. I had seen him a few days after I moved into the house. I watched him sitting on the open plaza above the Atlantic waves. I watched him from my balcony. He was a loner. It wasn't just that he was always on his own, no, he was a loner. I could tell by his demeanour: the way he walked, the way he sat, the way his eyes glazed as he looked over the sea. From up here in my eyrie I had spotted my prey. I strolled onto the plaza. He sat facing the sea. He looked unhappy. I saw him through my sunglasses looking at my red lipstick and my loose bottle-blond hair. And finally his eyes settled on my not insubstantial breasts, their fullness shown to advantage by an undone button. I reeled him in.
"I hope you're not thinking of jumping!"
We walked back to my green house together, arm in arm. He was in his mid-thirties, not to my taste but good looking in a rugged and very Latin way.

BALCONIES

"I have just moved in." We both spoke in English, a language foreign to both of us. "There are some boxes that need to be lifted. They are very heavy. You can help me. Then afterwards we can have some wine together. I have a much better view of the sea. From there, if you jump you'll be certain to end it all." There had been tears (so easy) and lots of wine (his neat, mine well watered) and he hadn't taken long to offer his help. God had guided me that day – he was the perfect accomplice, if a poor lover.
"No-one must know, Mateo." We hatched long into the night until the plan was clear. I simply threw in a comment here and there until he was convinced the idea was his own. It was a stroke of luck – thank you God – that he could lay his hands on a uniform. That would make it even simpler. The *sweet senorita* was the final touch. He loved the excitement of it: the plotting and planning; the spying; the murder.

That meeting with the boy in Taormina caught me off-guard. I was angry and in pain. Otherwise I might have been able to persuade him. He just turned up at the flat. I was still grieving for Tony. There hadn't been time for the red lips and the blond hair...
"We could be partners together – you and me." That's what he'd wanted from me – a partnership!
"And what would I be, Robbie? A sleeping partner?" And he'd laughed at the thought of that. An unpleasant laugh.

BALCONIES

"I wouldn't be averse to a bit of sleeping... But it's actually your money I want!"

"You're a blackmailing bastard. A greedy English bastard..." And I wished the words back into my throat as I saw his expression change. Suddenly he wanted more from me. Much much more!

"The price has gone up," he roared in my face. Then there was silence. When he'd arrived he would have settled for a bar in Sicily and a silent partner. Now he demanded a much bigger payout.

"In Tenerife. An Irish bar in Tenerife, that's what you'll get me. Or I'll go to the police and tell them what I saw."

I tried to change tack. I tried another way. But the lipstick didn't work this time and the tears were wasted.

"You're nothing but a murdering tart! And I'll get my money or you'll get what's coming to you." The meeting finished shortly after that... He left me to settle my affairs and fly out to Tenerife to meet him with a quarter of a million euros. Then I saw Mateo.

The three texts have been sent. The sim-card has been destroyed – flushed away. Things are in motion and before too long it will be over: the greedy boy with his nasty intentions; the ingénue, wearing her naiveté like a badge; and the Latin lover with his poor teeth and foolish dreams. Now there are things for me to prepare. I look around the living room.

BALCONIES

There is nothing here of mine. There is nothing to regret. What few possessions I have here are in my shoulder bag. Now I must simply be patient; it is almost time. The balcony invites me out again. The sun shines hot and yellow in a clear blue sky. The sea breaks noisily beneath me and I feel the spray as it crashes on the rocks below. Teide is clear too, though there are wispy clouds around its shoulders. The image reminds me of the coolness of the evening, and I grab a thin shawl to cover *my* shoulders. I check the mirror again and there she is, the grieving widow staring at me. In the kitchen there is one last thing to do before I am free again. By tonight it will all be over. Someone will get what's coming to them. That's for sure.

BALCONIES

DEPARTURES

The scrap of paper feels small in my hand, considering it holds my future. Walking down the seven flights to the pool balcony gives me time to think about it. The woman had not resisted. She had paid up as he had asked. The bikini girls are still there. As I pass they smile at me. They can already see a successful businessman. This is the new me, and they will all want a bit of it, even if it's just while they're on holiday.
"We're having a party tonight, in our apartment. And then, a midnight swim – skinny-dipping - down here. Are you up for

BALCONIES

it?" The middle bikini smiles at me and puts her drink on the white poolside table.

"I'm Irish. I'm always up for it. Ever-Ready Robbie, that's me. What time does it start?"

"As soon as you arrive, Robbie" the left bikini says and returns to her straw. She holds her hand out to me, and passes me a numbered key. "Let yourself in."

The right bikini gives me her empty glass. "We're going up soon to get ready. But I need another drink first, Robbie." As I take her glass to the poolside bar I hear them behind me, all giggles and whispers.

"A refill for the girl in the red bikini," I tell the waiter and he takes the glass, glances over at her and smiles at me.

"Si senor."

I look back and wave the key and all three raise their glasses. I try to imagine us all skinny dipping. That's easy dreaming! Business *and* pleasure; why not? A midnight swim will finish the day nicely. The watch says 7:35 and the light is fading fast.

Their conversation drifts over the patio and my plan is formed. It is all going *too* easily. It must be God's will. It's about time I got some of the luck. I watch him as he leaves, through the patio gate onto the main road down to the port. He is going to La Arena for our rendezvous. He's early. It's not yet eight o'clock; it's not yet dark. I follow him, down past the Post Office and the queue of tourists waiting at the bus stop. He

BALCONIES

doesn't turn round. He doesn't know he's being followed. The return journey will be his last. He is a young caballero on holiday with too much drink inside him, out to impress the pretty girls, taking a midnight swim... It's easy to be careless. He slows as he stops at the viewing point, a balcony overlooking the beach at Puerto Santiago. He stands like so many do looking down below at the beach and cafe a hundred feet below. His arms are on the silver bars and his body is bent forward as I pass him. It would be so easy to tip him right here. But no – there are plans in place. And we are not alone.

He looks at his watch, slowly stretches, smiles – at the thought of a midnight swim with three pretty girls, with a bag full of money? – and then he moves on round the serpentine corners until the Plaza Arena is in sight. He looks at his watch again. He knows he is early. He crosses the road. I know where he's going.

Past the Cantina Mexicana, there, below the street level is the old Highland Paddy. It's been closed for a while but this is my new place. I'll call it The Irish Harp and cold Guinness will be our speciality; yes, and exotic cocktails. I peer into the darkened windows. Through the grime are the remains of a bar. *My* bar, like a phoenix rising. I move back to the Cantina and go to the counter. It's still early so I have a choice of bar

BALCONIES

staff. I look at the pretty girl with the dark Spanish eyes. "Cerveza, per favor," and I point at the draught lager.

It's nearly time. He is over the road. In the darkness now I can see him, and his beer is almost finished. He pays the girl behind the bar, leaves the Cantina and crosses the road. The traffic is light. The daytime-resort bustle is finished and the night-time revels have not yet begun. He moves past without seeing me and jogs down the steps until he reaches the very edge of the Plaza, where the waves rush up to the cliffs a metre below. He sits in the very spot where I sat that day La Senora first spoke to me. La Senora! I make my way slowly to him and place the bag in front of him.
"Can I count it?"
I shrug my shoulders and take a cigarette from the packet he offers me. I pocket it while he unzips the bag and looks inside. I will smoke it later with her, after we have made love. People pass, some stop for photos, but I keep my back to them. I don't mind if they see him, but *I* don't want to be in any of their pictures.
"Tell her thanks. She won't be hearing from me again."

I zip the bag closed. I need a moment to recover. So much money and it's all mine. My Irish Harp is real. I can hear the plucking of its strings. I turn back to the man. He looks

BALCONIES

vaguely familiar but I don't know him. He is holding out his hand.

"The phone, senor." I pass him the mobile and I watch as he removes the card and hands it back to me.

"I don't want the phone..." but he is already moving away, back up to Los Gigantes. I sit for a moment. My throat is dry, my breathing is fast. Slowly, light-headed I stand. *That must be strong lager* I hear myself say. I look back up the hill which will take me back to Gigansol. I have a date now with three gorgeous girls. What could be better? I don't want to bump into him again so I'll stop off on the way at that bar alongside the beach at the Puerto. I saw it earlier on my way down and it looks the perfect place to sit and catch my breath. Instead of going up the hill and past the high balcony alongside the road, I turn left down the tiny lane that runs steeply downhill to the port. There are people there standing at the water's edge, just shadows under the string of lights that adorn the beach. Even in the darkness the water seems inviting. Over to my left is a diving board and I hear a loud splash and screams as someone dives into the sea. A man climbs out grabs a towel one of his friends hands him, and arms around each other's shoulders they come back towards me scrambling over the rocks. I hear their laughter and I laugh too. A swim will do me good.

BALCONIES

I can see him, even in the darkness, climbing over the rocks towards the diving board. He passes others who are returning. They are no more than silhouettes now but I recognise him, the bag attached to his arm like an extra limb. What could be simpler than an accident here on the rocks? It's not what we planned but how much simpler. It will take me five minutes to reach him.

The water is cold, as it splashes up over the rocks. Just a quick swim here to clear my head then another lager and I'll be ready for the Gigansol girls. I look around. There is no one. I have the place to myself. I strip off my shoes, socks, shirt, and shorts. Underpants will be fine. It's more than I'll have on later! I put the bag into a crevice in the black rocks and cover it with my discarded clothes. I pick my way along the water's edge to the diving board. I don't see him till it's too late. He has something in his hand and he raises it above my head. I feel the cold water at the same time as the jagged rocks against my head.

I pick my way back across the rocks; the bag is heavy and unbalances me. At last I'm on the pavement. I look back down. There is no one there and the only sound is the sea breaking against the rocks. There are no shouts for help. Nothing. The boy has learned his lesson. He will never again be able to threaten La Senora. She is free of him and I will be

BALCONIES

well rewarded. I lick my lips at the thought and taste the salt. Under a streetlamp I put the bag down and stand for a moment. It is a terrible thing I have done, but it was necessary. I will return the money to her and we shall drink long into the night. I pass the rendezvous Plaza and now there are more cars and La Cantina is noisy. The night shift has started. I climb the hill, move into the darkness of the driveway. The security lights don't come on as they usually do. The door is there and it is open for me. The kitchen light is on and the door leading onto the balcony is open. I put the bag onto the hall floor and I call out to her. Perhaps she is in the kitchen?

"La Senora?" I pull out the cigarette and feel for my lighter.

It is ten minutes since Mateo passed me, going back to the green house on the cliff. I handed back the keys this afternoon to the agent. It was no longer my home. This was no longer my island.

"The house was lovely – such a beautiful setting with a balcony over the Atlantic," I'd told the agent, "but I must return home. A family emergency." I signed the name I use on this island and deposited the keys.

What can he be doing? I left it all ready for him. It's time to go. I see the taxi turning round to collect me from my seat on the promenade. I have just a bag. Travelling light has become a habit. Of course I'll miss the money but it is a small price to

BALCONIES

pay for my freedom. The black-headscarfed woman who is leaving La Arena is nothing like the brash blond red-lipped woman that arrived a few months ago. I see the flash before I hear the bang, which coincides with my slam of the taxi door. The house explodes and if they look carefully enough the watchers will see a shower of euro notes. That's my gift to the island. Poor Mateo. He was not Tony. The first blue and white police cars flew past us before we had reached the main road that ran to the airport.

I am impatient. It is a fault. My parents always tell me. The Correos doesn't open until 8.30 in the morning and I arrived well before, while the gates were still locked. Now I am here at the counter among the first visitors. Mostly it's tourists clutching postcards but the man in front of me is holding a large package and I hope he isn't going to be an age. Typically, there is only one woman behind the counter. I can feel my feet moving and I play with the key between my fingertips. All I need to know is which of the boxes it will open. Then I shall be a thousand euros richer. There have been so many police cars. I saw their blue lights last night and they had set up a cordon, blocking the road just beyond my apartment block down from La Arena up the hill to La Puerto. Someone in the next-door apartment mentioned a gas explosion in a nearby house. When more police stop with a screech outside the only thing I think is perhaps they'll arrest the man in front of

BALCONIES

me for trying to send a package illegally. Then I can get to the front of the queue and open my box. One of the policemen takes my arm, then another pulls me out of the line. They snatch the key out of my hand. The Guardia who is clearly in charge of the locals takes the key, looks at it and gives it to another who goes into the lobby. The boxes stand in a row. The policeman with the key runs his eyes over them, finds the number he is looking for and opens it. Inside is a package. It's not my thousand euros. It's a white package bound roughly with brown parcel tape. I am bundled into the police car and a convoy follows me up towards the police station.

There are police surrounding the 'Tenerife Duty Free' shop at the airport. Passengers have been shepherded away and a policeman is questioning the manager. They will want to know more about the drug-smuggling senorita with the sweet smile. My plane departure gate flashes on the screen. It is time to leave.

BALCONIES

Acknowledgements are due to Linda, who shared the holiday in Malta and Tenerife that were the sources of inspiration.

I am also grateful to the members of Retford Authors Group, who enjoy my writing as much as their own, and who make good companions.

Other novels by Barry Upton:

Going Home

The Academy

St. Swithin's Day: I - Questor; II - New Order

Fugue

Sleeping

Lost and Found - short stories

Conquest: Three Historical Novels focused on the year 1066. I - Harald Hardrads; II - Harold Godwinson; III - William of Normandy (to be published in December 2024)

BALCONIES

Details of the earlier novels can be found on the website: https://barryuptonauthor.com or by scanning QR code below

What readers have said about earlier books:

A really enjoyable read...

The characters are clearly and realistically defined...

Astute understanding of the trauma of adolescence.

Thoroughly enjoyed reading this book...

Sometimes disturbing and sometimes sad but a gripping, well written book right from the start...

Hard to put down!

Please add your review on the Amazon site.

Printed in Great Britain
by Amazon